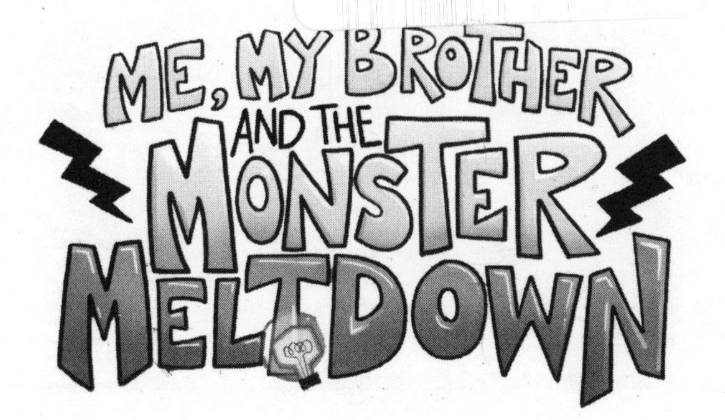
ME, MY BROTHER
AND THE
MONSTER
MELTDOWN

To Mum and Dad – RLJ
Just to Mum – Otis and Jago

For Joseph – AP

First published 2022 by Walker Books Ltd
87 Vauxhall Walk, London SE11 5HJ

2 4 6 8 10 9 7 5 3 1

This book has been typeset in Berkeley Oldstyle

Printed and bound by CPI Group (UK) Ltd, Croydon CR0 4YY

British Library Cataloguing in Publication Data:
a catalogue record for this book is
available from the British Library

ISBN 978-1-5295-0351-7

www.walker.co.uk

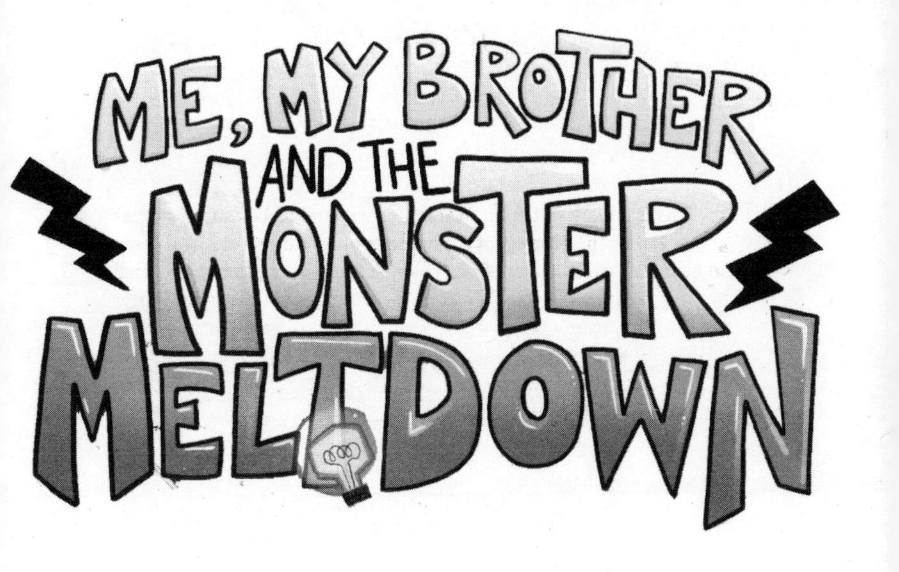

ROB LLOYD JONES

illustrated by Alex Patrick

WALKER
BOOKS

DaD
MUM
Otis
Jago
Daisy
Hardeep
Suzie
Ben

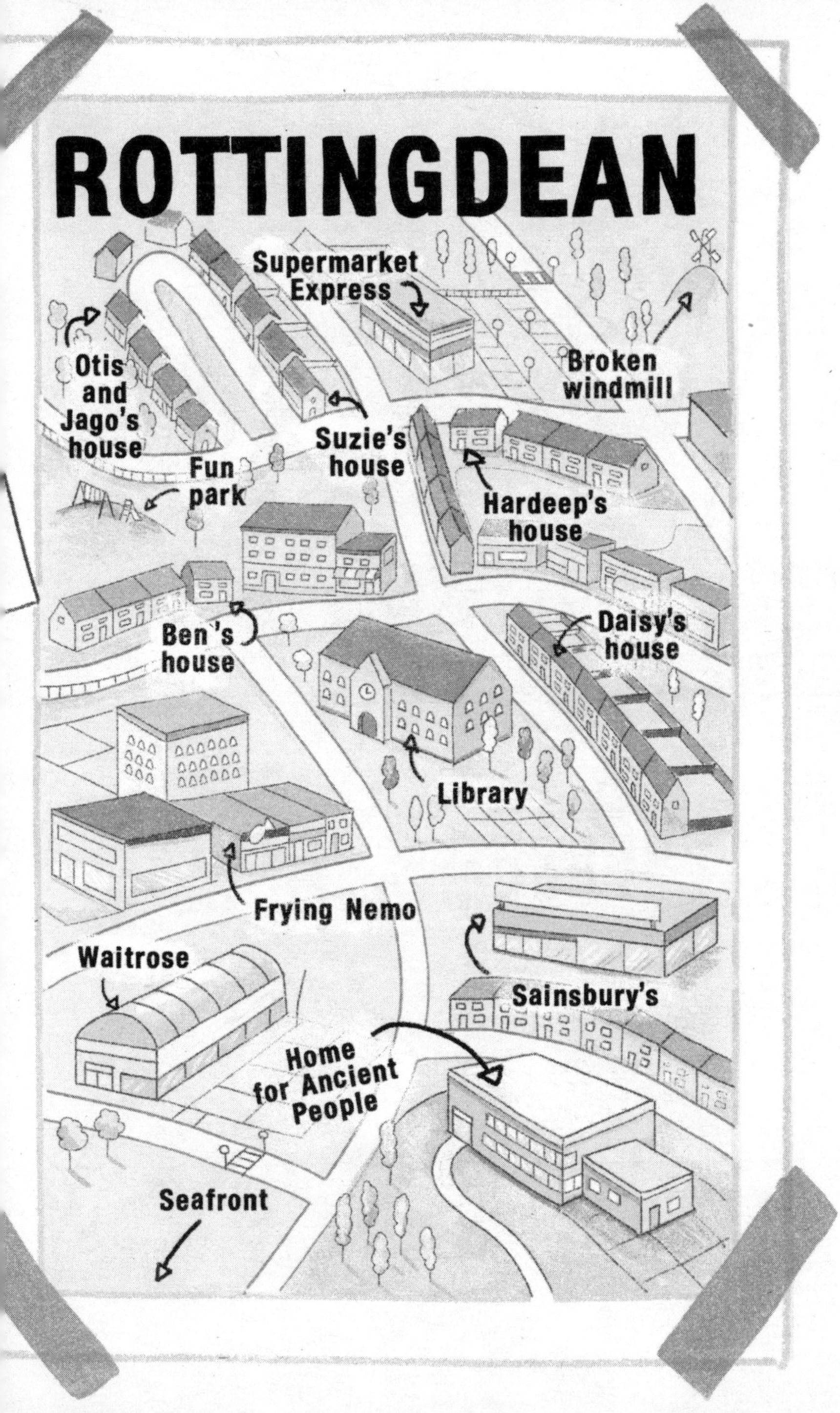

ROTTINGDEAN

Supermarket Express

Otis and Jago's house

Broken windmill

Suzie's house

Fun park

Hardeep's house

Ben's house

Daisy's house

Library

Frying Nemo

Waitrose

Sainsbury's

Home for Ancient People

Seafront

SALE
SUPERM
RKET
EXPRESS
CORN POPS

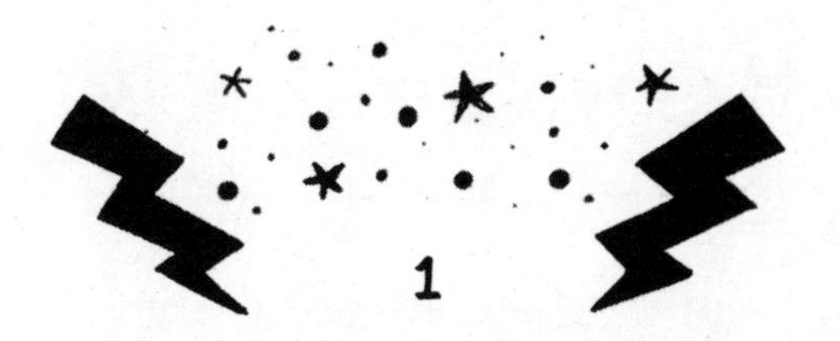

1

ALL THE ADULTS ARE FREAKING OUT

I knew something weird was going on when the six-headed gingerbread man smashed up our local Tesco.

The mega biscuit monster was the size of a skyscraper, with icing cuffs and Jelly Tot buttons bigger than small cars. Well, about the size of big cars, really. According to the news, it blasted the baking aisle with lightning bolts from its gingerbread hands, grinning weirdly the whole time.

Maybe it would have destroyed the other aisles too, but the Army sent in soldiers and they blew it into a pile of crumbs. Army scientists ran around collecting the biscuit bits in special bags, but old Mrs Liphook found a piece they'd missed in the car park and took it home to dunk it in a cup of tea. Mum said that

was a dumb thing to do and we should stay away from her in case she turns into a mutant monster, too.

Loads of stuff like that has been happening lately.

Three weeks ago, a giant part-shrimp-part-lion-part-peacock creature appeared in Brighton and blew up an Aldi with laser

zaps from its knees. Since then, freaky monsters have smashed up supermarkets in loads of towns and villages close to Rottingdean, which is where we live. The TV news even thinks the monsters may be targeting Rottingdean, although no one knows why. It's a pretty tiny town with the sea on one side and big chalky hills called the Downs on the other, and not much else really. It's got a lot of old people, a windmill that doesn't work, a fish and chip shop called Frying Nemo and a fun park – which isn't really a park, just a slide and swing, and where no one's ever had any fun. Well, apart from my friend Suzie Grotwood, who goes there to practise burping the whole alphabet in one go so she can get onto *Britain's Got Talent*.

The only unusual thing about Rottingdean is that it has a lot of supermarkets. Like, way more than it needs. You can't leave the town in any direction without passing one, and people come from all along the coast to shop in them. That used to be a really good thing because all the local adults have jobs in them, including my dad. But now it's not such a good thing because it seems to have made our town the centre of a Monster Apocalypse.

Ever since the giant gingerbread man incident in Tesco, all the adults have been freaking out. Dad has turned our basement into a survival bunker, filling it with tins of baked beans he bought with his work discount. Baked beans! That's all we'll eat during the end of the world.

Mum has started praying to every god from every religion, including the ancient ones. She's convinced one of them is punishing us but she doesn't know which. That's like 12,000 gods, so it takes her most of the day to do all the prayers. Dad says if a god wanted to punish us, why would it send flying jellyfish with googly eyes?

There have been loads of other monsters since then, too. They're totally random, except for one common theme: they all hate supermarkets. Just in the last few days, in and around Rottingdean…

* Sixty pink pandas (with bits of broccoli sprouting from their heads) pounded a Sainsbury's.
* A gigantic neon poo emoji (with vampire fangs) pulverized a Co-op.
* An enormous, bouncing bum (with a huge, creepy grin) destroyed a Budgens that they tried to disguise as a cinema but somehow the monster knew.

Scientists gave them boring names, but "Unspecified Destructive Entity No. 62" really was just a massive pink butt. It bounced through Brighton, crushing cars on its way to Waitrose. People said it grinned at them each time it bounced up. Apparently, one time it did a fart so

loud that the pennies finally fell from the shelves in the slot machines on the pier. It bounced to Waitrose, and then bounced up and down *on* Waitrose until the supermarket was totally smashed up. By the time it was finished, the fog of fart gas was so thick that a news reporter puked her guts out on live TV.

The giant butt had bounced off by the time the Army turned up. It was last spotted headed into the Downs, and no one's seen it since. Monsters that escape are never seen again. Sometimes they *actually* vanish. One moment they're smashing up supermarkets and then they're gone. It's one of the Big Mysteries about the **UNSPECIFIED DESTRUCTIVE ENTITIES**.

But it's not the REALLY WEIRD thing.

The really weird thing about the giant gingerbread man – the thing that made me spit out my squash when I heard it on the news – was that it had *six heads*.

Gingerbread men do not usually have

six heads. I know this because when I eat them, I always bite the head off first, and there's only ever one. Unless I steal my brother's biscuit... But that's not the point. Another proof is that in the story of the runaway gingerbread man, he DOES NOT sing, "Run, run, as fast as you can, you can't catch me, I'm the six-headed gingerbread man."

Why would a gingerbread man need six heads?

Dad suggested that maybe where giant living gingerbread men come from, six heads is normal, but no one knows *where* the monsters come from.

The prime minister gathered an **ELITE TEAM** of scientists to work it out. He gave them a long and serious name –

the **B**ureau for the

Investigation of

Giant

Beasts and

Unexplained

Monsters

– but didn't realize until later that the initials spell **BIGBUM**, so that's what everyone calls them.

BIGBUM put up posters along the coast telling us not to panic. One of them said,

DON'T PANIC!

Another said,

EVERYTHING IS FINE!

A third said,

IF YOU SEE A MONSTER, CURL UP INTO A LITTLE BALL AND SCREAM, OR RUN AROUND IN CIRCLES WITH YOUR ARMS IN THE AIR (BUT DON'T PANIC).

The prime minister is on TV every day, speeching about not panicking. But the broadcasts always come from the government's secret underground survival bunker, and sometimes he starts sobbing and pulling his hair in the middle of his speech, so I guess he's not really *not panicking*, either.

All the adults are freaking out about the Monster Apocalypse. But everyone is so *busy* freaking out that no one's stopped to think about the actual monsters doing the apocalypsing.

Why would a giant gingerbread man have six heads?

No one has asked that.

Well, I didn't need to. The moment I heard about it, I knew the answer.

The giant gingerbread man has six heads because that's how my brother drew it.

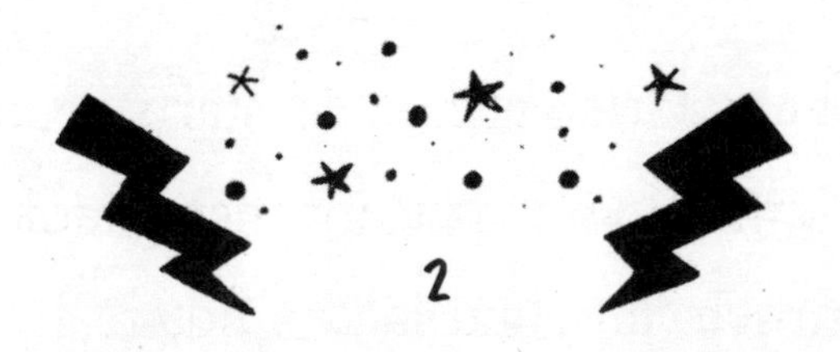

2

SOME THINGS YOU SHOULD KNOW ABOUT JAGO

Here are some things you should know about my little brother Jago:

* He thinks he's a punk rocker. He doesn't even know what a punk rocker is, but he heard the words once and liked them and decided he was one. If you ask him what that means, he'll say it's his job but he'll dodge explaining what it involves.
* He is six years old.
* He likes dancing. A lot. If any music

of any form is playing in any place, turn around and Jago will be dancing.

- He is not a very good dancer. Mostly he just thrashes his head and swings his arms. Dad said once that when Jago dances, he looks like a windmill in a hurricane. Jago always says, "See? That's what punk rockers do."

- He is almost always happy.
- When he is not happy, he is *ultra* not happy. Like the monsters, he stomps

around and smashes things up. It takes ages for Mum to stop him crying because his breathing goes funny and he can't calm down even with his asthma puffer. He once cried so hard that he pooed himself – an actual poo came out! But we never mention it in case it sets him off again.

* When he grows up, he wants to be a scientist, a dancer, a ninja and a blacksmith. All at the same time.
* He likes licking the froth off the top of coffee.
* He follows me around and copies what I do.
* He hates supermarkets.
* He draws things.

3

A MASSIVE NON-COINCIDENCE

I don't know why my brother draws so much, because he's not particularly good and he never gets any better.

All the schools shut when the apocalypse began, in case a monster smashed them up on the way to a supermarket. So Mum and Dad have to homeschool us while they work from home. I mean *have to* because they don't *want to.* They take turns and whoever's turn it is spends most of the time yelling,

"It's your turn now!" at the other person.

They are *rubbish* at homeschooling, too. Mum stares at the work set by my school and mutters that "This isn't how they did things when I was young..." Then she runs to the stairs and shouts to Dad that it's his turn.

Dad is even worse. He reminds us not to panic about the apocalypse almost every minute.

"Don't panic," he says. "Otis, are you panicking? Jago, stop panicking!"

We never *are* panicking. Usually, we're watching cartoons.

Then he charges across the room, waving his arms and

yelling, "OH MY GOSH, WHAT ARE THESE THINGS AND WHY ARE THEY HERE?!"

The other day he charged straight into a wall and knocked himself out. I shouted to Mum, who shouted back that it was still Dad's turn so we should just leave him there and get on with something.

So we did what we usually do when Mum and Dad are going nuts.

We drew stuff.

We draw a lot, my brother and me, and all over the place. Sometimes we lie on the trampoline and draw, sometimes we draw at the kitchen table and sometimes we draw *on* the table, although we always have to scrub it off. But the things we draw aren't quite the same. My drawings are a bit weird, but Jago's are just properly demented.

THREE THINGS I DREW RECENTLY:

A manga ninja assassin

A musketeer with a twirly moustache that goes "twang" when he plucks it

A weird crocodile

THREE THINGS JAGO DREW RECENTLY:

A part-shrimp-part-lion-part-peacock monster with neon rays spurting from its knees

A massive bouncing butt

A giant grinning gingerbread man … with six heads

You may recognize two of those?

I didn't work it out when I heard about the bouncing butt in Brighton, because the **BIGBUM** scientists didn't call it a butt. They called it a "bispherical fleshy sentient being", or a "peach-shaped creature with distinctive central opening".

I know *now* that one of those means "big thinking butt" and the other means "big bum with obvious bumhole", but at the time I didn't get it.

Then came the gingerbread man…

It was a massive non-coincidence. I spat out my squash (orange and mango) and spluttered something like, "What – no – wait – hang on – no – wait – what?"

Dad hurled his newspaper in the air and screamed, "WHAT IS IT? IS THERE ONE COMING? GET IN FRONT OF ME!"

I didn't want him running into any more walls, so I said I needed a poo and dashed off. But now I was freaking out, too, as I raced up to the bedroom I share with Jago. I leaped onto the bottom bunk, Jago's bed, my heart beating so hard I thought I might puke. Then my heart seemed to stop as I found what I was looking for.

Something Jago drew on the bed frame.

A six-headed gingerbread man.

It looked exactly the same as the monster that pulverized Tesco. I mean *exactly* the same. Same crazy red grin, same six heads (each one smaller than the last, as Jago was running out of space on the shoulders) and the same jagged yellow lines blasting from its hands.

Lightning bolts.

It *was* the monster.

Only, Jago drew it two days ago, before he'd ever heard about the Tesco pulverizer. Before *anyone* had ever heard about it, or seen it.

Just like the bouncing butt.

Was he ... somehow ... *causing* all this?

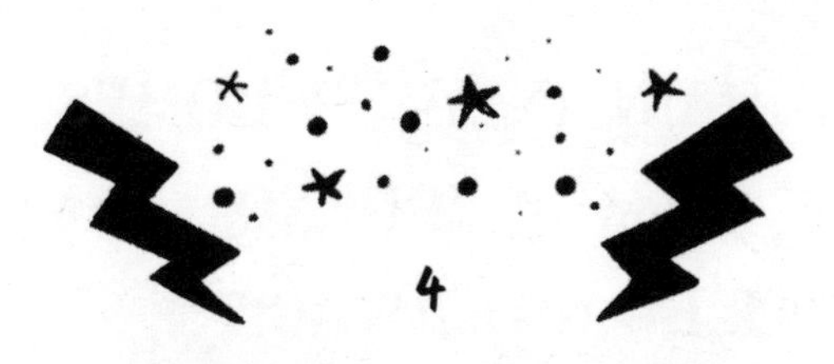

4

SEVERAL THOUSAND CAUSES FOR ALARM

"ATTENTION, ALL CITIZENS!"

This didn't sound good.

"I REPEAT: ATTENTION, ALL CITIZENS!"

Dad said that if anyone ever called us "citizens", something bad was about to happen. Now a soldier was yelling it through a megaphone, from inside an army jeep that was rumbling down our cul-de-sac.

I leaped from the bed and pelted down the stairs, taking them four at a time.

"REMAIN IN YOUR HOMES!" the soldier bellowed. **"DO NOT PANIC! I REPEAT: DO NOT PANIC!"**

Too late. Dad was already in full-blown panic mode, charging about, flapping his arms as he wailed at us to get into the survival bunker.

Mum yelled back as she typed frantically on her laptop. "It's a survival *basement*, John. And there's no Wi-Fi down there. I have a three p.m. Zoom meeting for work."

"A Zoom meeting?" Dad cried. "Jane, this is the end of the world!"

"THIS IS *NOT* THE END OF THE WORLD!" hollered the soldier in the jeep, as if he could hear my parents' argument. **"SOME PARTS OF THE WORLD ARE EXPECTED TO SURVIVE!"**

"Jago," Dad snapped, "get into the survival bunker."

Jago looked up from his sketch pad, and the drawing he was doing. "Can't."

"Why not?"

"Don't like baked beans."

"Get the cheese, then!" Dad shot back. "We can have cheese and beans!"

"No cheese grater in the bunker, either," Jago muttered, returning to his scribbles.

"Or Wi-Fi," Mum added. "How can a survival basement not have Wi-Fi?"

Dad was about to reply but he ran into a wall again and collapsed on the carpet. I had no idea what was going on, and none of my family were in any state to explain, so I snatched Dad's phone from his pocket and checked the news.

It was on every website.

Vast numbers of Unspecified Destructive Entities appear over English Channel!

"DO NOT PANIC!" the solider repeated.

I threw open the front door, watching the jeep trundle by on its way to the end of our cul-de-sac.

"THERE IS NO CAUSE FOR ALARM!" the voice boomed from the megaphone.

"What about all the monsters?" I shouted.

"OK, THERE IS *ONE* CAUSE FOR ALARM," admitted the voice from the jeep.

"The news says there are loads of them," I replied.

"FAIR ENOUGH, THERE ARE LOADS OF CAUSES FOR ALARM."

"Like, several thousand."

"ALL RIGHT, THERE ARE SEVERAL THOUSAND CAUSES FOR ALARM. BUT DO NOT BE ALARMED."

Jago came up beside me, his sketch-book dangling from his hand. "Our dad just ran into a wall!" he yelled.

"DADS DO THAT," the soldier replied.

"All of them?"

"PRETTY MUCH."

The jeep reached the end of the cul-de-sac and began an awkward attempt to turn. All the neighbours were watching, but they seemed more concerned about the jeep scratching their cars than the soldier's warnings. Old Mrs Liphook eyed the army vehicle with particular suspicion. Her mouth screwed up like a gooseberry.

"Don't you dare drive over those daffodils!" she snapped. "What sort of monsters are they this time, anyway?"

"I AM NOT AT LIBERTY TO DISCLOSE THAT INFORMATION, MADAM,"

the jeep voice replied. **"HOWEVER, IF YOU HAPPEN TO HAVE ANTI-AIRCRAFT DEFENCES, NOW WOULD BE A GOOD TIME TO DEPLOY THEM."**

"I have an electric fly swatter," Mrs Liphook muttered.

"GRAB IT."

I snatched Jago's sketchbook from his hand and stared at his latest scribbled drawing.

"Mr Army Person?" I yelled. "Are the monsters flying great white sharks with big green lips, and eyes that blast pink laser beams?"

The jeep halted its attempt to turn between Mrs Liphook's daffodil patch and Mr Strachan's mobility scooter, which he'd refused to move. The jeep door swung open and a soldier climbed out. He had silver hair and a face with lots of lines on it, like an old man's hand.

He marched over to us. "How did you know that, son?" he demanded.

I thrust the sketch pad at his face, pointing to Jago's drawing. It was the monster I'd just described.

"This is my brother," I added, as Jago came alongside me. "These are his drawings."

"Hello," said Jago. "Can I drive your jeep?"

"Sure," the soldier said. "Can't see any harm in that."

He was about to hand Jago the keys, but I jabbed at the sketchbook with my finger, forcing him to look at the drawings.

I explained how each of the creatures Jago had drawn had recently appeared somewhere close by and smashed up a supermarket. I told him that Jago hated supermarkets, too, and that I thought the monsters were his drawings come to life.

The soldier listened very carefully. "Fascinating," he said, finally. "We need

to take this information to military high command, who will treat the matter as an absolute priority. This could be the key to saving thousands, if not millions, of lives, and perhaps even— ”

He looked at his watch. “Ooh, time's up.”

“What?”

He turned and marched off. “I've finished for the day.”

“Wait!” I cried. “What about the drawings? And the military high command stuff?”

“Oh, yeah! Good luck with that,” he called.

And then he was gone. He'd even left his jeep, which Mrs Liphook was whacking with her fly swatter because it had crushed a few of her daffodils. Maybe more soldiers would come to get it, and I could talk to them instead? But how long would that take?

The flying sharks were on their way!

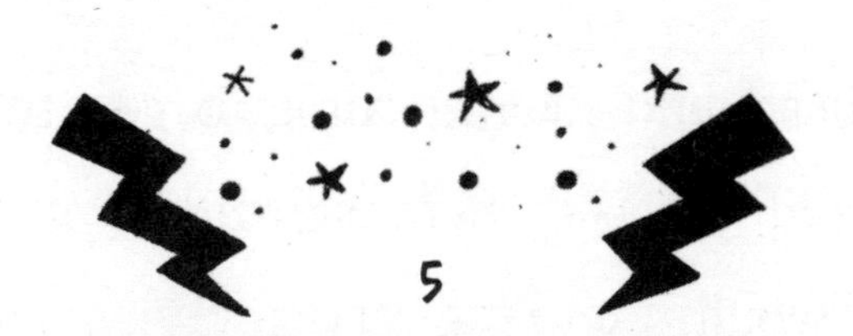

THE CLICKER PEN

So Mum and Dad were going crazy, the Army had gone home for a nap and there were thousands of flying great white sharks with laser-blasting eyes heading for Rottingdean.

This was NOT GOOD.

My brother had turned the radio on and was now "punk rocking" around the living room, thrashing his head and playing air guitar to music that really wasn't rock music.

"Jago, listen to me very carefully," I said.

"OK."

"Are you listening very carefully?"

"Yep."

"You're not even looking at me. You're dancing."

"I can dance and listen."

"OK. See this sketchbook?"

"Yeah."

"You're still not looking at it."

"It is *my* sketchbook, Otis. I know what it looks like."

"So you remember the drawings of all these weird monsters?"

"Yeah, sure."

"Please stop dancing and look!"

Out of breath, he stared at his sketch pad as I flicked through its pages. There was no point showing Mum and Dad. They were too busy panicking to listen and, anyway, they'd think that Jago drew the monsters *after* he'd seen them on the news. Only I knew that he had drawn each monster *before* it appeared. He'd somehow made his drawings come to life. But how?

Maybe it was one of the thousands of gods Mum had been praying to every day? No, she began praying *after* the monsters first appeared. Perhaps some sort of magical creature was to blame? But which? There were hundreds!

I turned to the first drawing on the pad – the part-shrimp-part-lion-part-

peacock with neon rays spurting from its knees. It was the first monster that appeared, three weeks ago.

"Jago, did anything strange happen when you drew this?"

"What like?"

"Did a wizard cast a spell on you?"

"Which wizard?"

"Any wizard."

"I don't know any wizards. Do you?"

I thought about it. "I don't think so. Maybe a wizard walked by the house randomly casting spells?"

"We live in a cul-de-sac."

That was a good point. Ours was the third last house in the close – no one went past other than Mrs Liphook or Mr Strachan, and I was fairly sure neither of them was a wizard or a genie.

Dad was still unconscious on the carpet after running into the wall, so we took his phone and looked up a list of magical creatures. We studied pictures of dwarfy gnomes, unicorns and fairies, magical eels, mystical dragons, a shapeshifting toad, a ghostly whale skeleton…

My hopes rose as Jago had a long look at the ghostly whale skeleton. He grinned, then grabbed his favourite pen and began to sketch the creature on his pad.

"That's so cool—" he said.

"Wait!" I cried, snatching the pen and causing him to yelp. "You can't draw anything else!" I insisted. "There are already thousands of flying sharks heading our way. We can't add ghostly whale skeletons or … or…"

I stared at the pen I'd swiped from my brother's hand. It was one of those biros with a clicker at the end to choose between different colours of ink. Jago had used this pen to draw *all* of the weird creatures in his pad. Was it possible…?

"Jago, perhaps it's this pen. Maybe this *pen* is magical, not you. We have to find out why, and stop it."

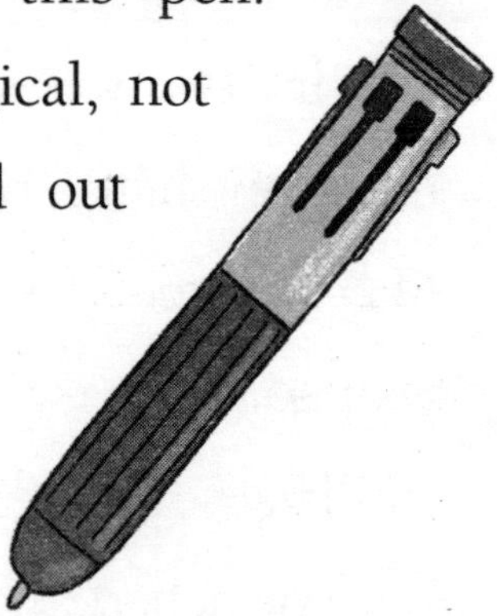

"That sounds dangerous," Jago replied. "Let's go!"

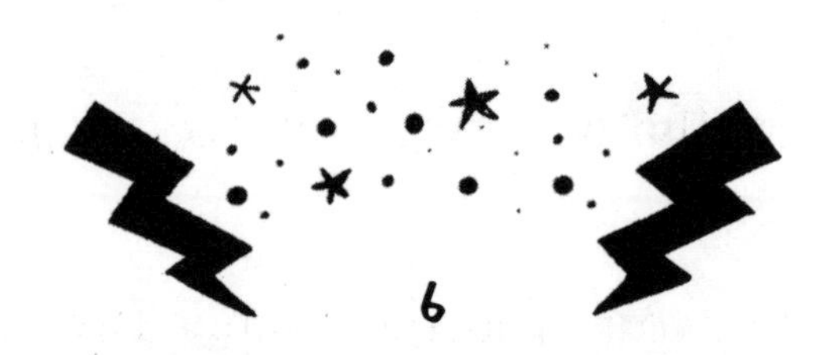

6

MRS GROTWOOD GOES ALL WEIRD

"Hello, Mrs Grotwood. Could we speak to Suzie, please?"

Mrs Grotwood stared at us and then burst out laughing. Only, it didn't sound like a proper laugh. It sounded like she was *making* herself laugh. She wasn't even smiling – not really, anyway. Her teeth were clenched and her lips trembled from the effort of forcing them open.

Then she shot out a hand and grabbed my nose. "Ha ha, you got me!"

she spluttered. "You pranked me good! Ha ha!"

She swore, and then yanked my nose even harder. "Sorry, I shouldn't swear, but you'll bleep that out for the show, won't you? Where are the cameras?"

"What cameras?" I groaned. "Please stop pulling my nose, Mrs Grotwood!"

"It's a mask! You can't fool me! You're TV presenters! You're Ant and Dec!"

"We're Otis and Jago! We go to school with Suzie."

She let go of my face and stepped back. Her smile was gone. Her lips screwed up like she'd just licked a cat poo.

"Oh. Are you sure you're not Ant and Dec?"

"I don't even know who they are," I moaned, clutching my nose. "That reference is completely lost on me."

"I might be Ant and Dec," Jago said.

"No, you're not," I insisted, because Mrs Grotwood's hand was twitching and I feared she might grab Jago's nose next. "We've come to see Suzie," I added.

She eyed us for another long moment,

and then sighed. "OK, but keep it brief. I'm expecting Ant and Dec."

She called for Suzie, who came down the stairs drinking a can of lemonade. She held up a hand, signalling for us to shut up and listen, and then began burping the alphabet. She got to the letter "T" before her face went sort of purple and she ran out of burp.

"Almost there," she gasped.

We congratulated her on how well she was doing.

"Why did your mum pull my nose?" I asked.

"Oh, she does that to everyone these days. The postman has stopped delivering our letters because of it."

"Huh?"

"In her mind, it's all a trick – all the monsters and stuff."

"So she doesn't believe any of this is really happening?"

Suzie shrugged. "Nope. She thinks she's being set up on one of those TV prank shows and that everyone who knocks on the door is the presenter wearing a mask. That's why she pulled your nose – to check if you were real. What are you doing here, anyway?"

"We need to ask about a pen you gave Jago at his birthday party." I showed her Jago's clicker pen. "Do you remember where you got it?"

She squinted at the biro and nodded. "Hardeep Khan gave it to me for my birthday and I regifted it. Why do you want to know?"

"We're on a quest to stop the end of the world."

"That sounds dangerous. Can I come?"

"Sure."

Suzie grinned, and shouted to her mum. "Mum, I'm going with Otis and Jago to stop the end of the world."

Somewhere inside the house, Suzie's mum erupted in more manic laughter. "Ha ha, oh yes, of course you are, darling. Good luck with that."

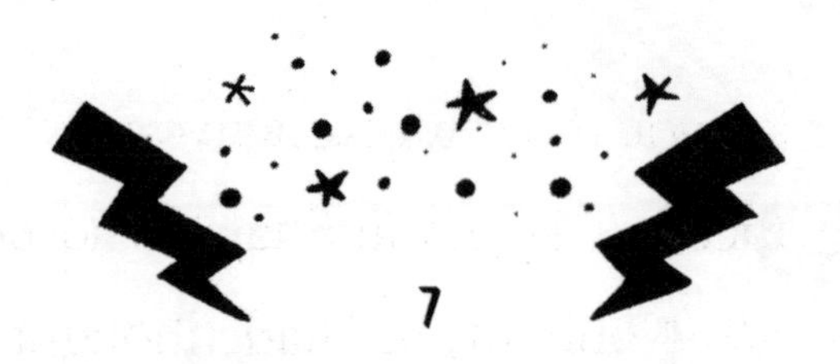

7

FINGER UP HIS NOSE

"Hello, Mr Khan. Is Hardeep in?"

Mr Khan's bushy eyebrows rose at the ends, like two caterpillars squaring up for a fight. I think it was his "suspicious glare".

"Who are you?" he snapped.

"Otis and Jago Jones, and this is Suzie Grotwood."

"We go to school with Hardeep," Suzie added.

Mr Khan folded his arms and snorted. "Prove it."

"Eh?"

"Prove you're who you say you are."

I glanced at Jago and Suzie, who both shrugged. None of us had thought to bring any form of identification. In fact, none of us *had* any form of identification.

"Monsters wear disguises, too," Mr Khan added.

"I don't think they do, Mr Khan," Suzie said.

Mr Khan snorted so hard that hairs sprang from his nostrils. "Course they do," he huffed. "Do you really believe the attackers actually look like that? They're clearly wearing disguises."

"What do they look like under their disguises?" Jago asked.

"No idea," he replied. "Maybe like you three."

"So you think all the monsters are, in fact, children in disguise?" I asked.

Mr Khan's eyebrows sank back down, and he sighed. "No, probably not," he admitted.

"Bit of a silly thing to say, wasn't it?" Suzie said.

"Mmm-hmm," Mr Khan agreed. "Truth is, this Monster Apocalypse thing is getting to me a bit."

"It's OK," Suzie said. "All the adults are freaking out. Anyway, we're on a dangerous quest to stop it all."

His eyebrows shot up again, but this time with surprise. "Oh, really? Well, I'll get Hardeep. He loves that sort of thing. Just to warn you, he has a finger stuck up his nose."

A moment later, Hardeep appeared with a finger stuck up his nose.

"Hi, Hardeep," Jago said. "What's up?"

"Finger … up … nose," he mumbled.

"How'd that happen?" I asked.

Hardeep shrugged, but we all knew the answer. He loves eating his own bogeys. Sometimes he skips school lunch because he's "already full up". Our teacher, Mrs Silverhorn, always warned him that if he kept picking his nose, his finger would get stuck up there. I guess it had finally happened.

It took a while to sort it out, with me and Suzie pulling and Jago bashing the back of his head like a ketchup bottle, but eventually Hardeep's finger popped out with an absolutely mega bogey on the end, which Hardeep popped in his mouth for a snack.

"Thanks, guys," he said, chewing. "So, what's up?"

I showed him the clicker pen. “Do you know where this pen came from?”

“Yep. Got it from Ben Tucker. It was a regift.”

“You mean you regifted a regift?”

“Yep. What’re you up to anyway?”

“We’re on a quest to save the world.”

“Sounds dangerous. Can I come?”

“Sure.”

Anyway, this went on all morning. Jago had been given the clicker pen by Suzie Grotwood, who was regifted it by Hardeep Khan, who’d got it from Ben Tucker, who said *he’d* got it from Daisy Horwitz. By lunchtime, there were six of us, and we still didn’t know where the pen had come from originally, why it had magic powers or how to stop them.

And we were running out of time!

(Because of the flying sharks that were on their way, I mean. It just didn't sound so dramatic to add that bit.)

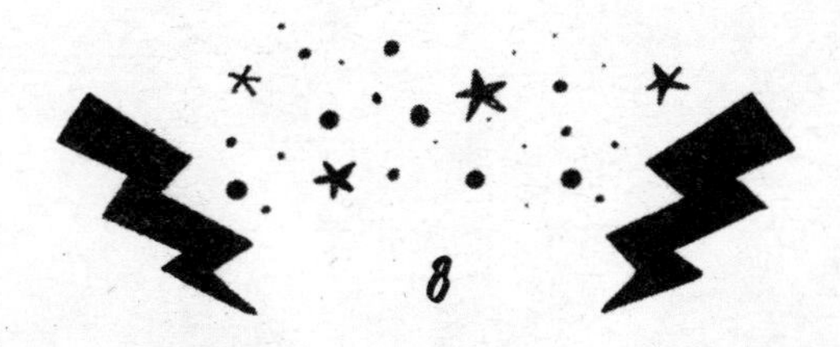

8

STRANGE SCIENTIFIC DEVICE

According to the news, the flying sharks were only five miles from the coast, so they'd be over Rottingdean really soon. Adults were still panicking all over the place. Some were stuffing their cars with suitcases, getting ready to flee. A few were sitting on the pavement sobbing. Others were fighting outside shops to get loo rolls. The world was about to end and they were worried about how they'd wipe their bums.

Apparently, the prime minister had

addressed the nation from his bunker, but he didn't say much and seemed to be pulling clumps of his hair out. The Army were still patrolling the streets in their jeeps, calling everyone "citizen" and telling us to stay in our house unless our house was destroyed by flying sharks with laser-beam eyes, in which case we should probably leave.

Us kids hid every time the Army drove

past, because we weren't meant to be outside. But hiding had got trickier as our group grew bigger. Six kids can't squeeze into a telephone box, even by climbing on top of each other. We did try once but we ended up tumbling out across the pavement, making us even more obvious to the jeep we'd been trying to hide from.

"Hey, you children!" the driver yelled.

The jeep skidded to a stop and a woman with a bushy grey beard got out. She spent a while fiddling with her trousers, then waddled over to us, shuffling awkwardly, as if she'd pooed her pants. She carried a strange scientific device, like a giant walkie-talkie, with a long antenna sticking from the top.

We thought about scarpering but decided to stay put. She didn't look like a soldier – and she seemed to really want to talk to us. Maybe she had information about the Monster Apocalypse.

"My name is Professor Spitbrick," she said as she waddled closer. "And, as you can see, I work for **BIGBUM**."

When she said "as you can see", she

turned so we could see her bum. It was actually huge – really massive and lumpy, like a sack stuffed with porridge.

"I thought you were called **BIGBUM** because it stood for something?" Suzie asked.

"A common misunderstanding," the professor replied. "It's because of the size of our buttocks. The acronym is entirely coincidental."

I didn't believe her. Her giant buttocks didn't even look real. I reckoned she'd stuffed pillows down the back of her trousers when she got out of the jeep. She just didn't want people thinking she hadn't realized her organization's initials spelled **BIGBUM**.

She held her strange scientific device out for us to see. "'What's this strange scientific device?' you ask," she said.

"No, we didn't," replied Ben Tucker.

The professor grinned. "Aha! Good question! Well, this here is an **SSD**."

"What does that stand for?"

"**Strange Scientific Device**," the professor explained. "It senses sources of unnatural power. Usually it detects **Unspecified Destructive Entities**, but for some reason it's reacting to you."

"Not us," squeaked Hardeep Khan. "It's Jago's pen."

Jago pushed to the front of the group

and raised his clicker pen. “This is the pen that’s drawn all the monsters,” he declared proudly.

I thought she might laugh at us, but instead her eyes went all squinty and she waved the **Strange Scientific Device** around Jago’s pen. The machine **BEEPED**, and her eyes went even squintier.

“Tell me everything,” she insisted.

So we did. It took a bit of time because we were all talking over each other, and most of our gang didn’t actually know *everything*, so they kept making stuff up. The professor raised her eyebrows and scratched her beard, and Jago held his pen up higher so she could scan it again with her strange scientific device.

Then she muttered, “How extraordinary.”

"So you believe us, then?"

"Not a word of it, no. But it's a fun little story."

She waddled off, holding up her trousers to keep the pillows in.

"Wait!" I shouted. "Do you think we can stop the Monster Apocalypse?"

She stopped and looked back. "Why are you asking *me*?"

"Because you're a scientist," Hardeep replied.

She looked surprised at that. "Oh, yes, I suppose I am. Well then, I would say the monsters will most likely either wipe out the human race or take us as slaves to build temples in whatever dimension they come from. Toodle-oo!"

Some of our group muttered mean

things about her, but I was delighted. I hadn't been totally sure about the pen – but now it had been confirmed by a genuine **Strange Scientific Device**! We really were onto something.

9

WHAT POLICE OFFICERS KEEP UNDER THEIR HATS

I honestly don't know how five people can regift the same clicker pen.

Five birthday parties. Five sheets of wrapping paper. Five kids opening the same present and not really wanting it. Five mums or dads deciding it wasn't a good-enough present to keep, but it was worth giving to someone else. But finally, we were reaching the end of the hunt, as we walked from Daisy Horwitz's house to her gran's care home, where her gran had won the pen in a Christmas raffle.

The care home is on the road out of Rottingdean, so we had to walk up the hill to get there. From halfway up, we could see across the town to the sea, and all the chaos going on. We counted twenty-six army trucks and jeeps, sixteen helicopters and eight massive cannons pointed to the sky. There were hundreds of soldiers, and more police cars and vans than we could count. Sirens were flashing and alarms were wailing, and everyone was just going totally nuts.

Then, as we got even higher, two fighter jets blasted over us. They were headed out over the sea, towards a thick dark cloud that was moving slowly towards the land.

Only, it wasn't a cloud.

"The flying great white sharks with laser-beam eyes..." Suzie said.

"Cool," Jago replied.

I guess it must be quite cool to see your own drawings come to life, but Jago was the only one grinning. The Army guy hadn't exaggerated. There were thousands of the monsters flying this way.

"Hey! Hey, you kids!"

Sergeant Snelling, the local police officer, sped towards us on his electric scooter. He wore one of those old-fashioned police helmets that made him seem taller than us, even though he was actually pretty short. He propped his scooter against a wall and strode over.

"You lot should be at home," he said. "Don't you know the world is about to end?"

"Doesn't really matter if we're at home or not, then, does it?" replied Ben Tucker, who was genius at being cheeky to adults.

Sergeant Snelling smiled. "Don't you kids worry, though. We have it all under control."

"You do?" I asked.

"Of course we do," he replied. "We're the police. We know how to handle a crisis. In fact, we're trained in all sorts of monster defence strategies."

"You are?" Hardeep asked.

"Course we are, sonny." He patted his helmet and grinned. "Why do you think I'm wearing this big old helmet?"

"Because it makes you look taller?" Suzie suggested.

"Ah, a common misconception,"

Snelling said. "No, in fact, I keep something under here. Something vital in the battle against these monsters. Look, I'm not meant to show you, but since you asked..."

"We didn't ask," Ben Tucker said.

Ignoring him, Sergeant Snelling began to remove his helmet,

careful not to dislodge whatever was hidden underneath. Slowly, he lifted the helmet away.

"Eh?" he said. He looked massively chuffed with himself. "How about that, then?"

We all stared.

"There's nothing there," I said.

His smile wobbled. He reached up and patted the top of his head, and his face turned as white as a really white ghost.

"Oh sugar ..." he rasped, "I left it at home again!"

He turned, sprinted to his scooter and zoomed off full pelt down the hill.

"All the adults do is freak out," Suzie muttered as we watched him go. "And those flying sharks are getting closer."

10
DAISY DRAWS A FART

As we carried on up the hill towards the care home, the two fighter planes roared over our heads. They were headed out to sea to take on the flying sharks.

"Could be worse," Suzie said.

"How?" I asked.

"I'd have drawn sabre-toothed tigers," she replied, and we all agreed that flying sharks with laser eyes were probably better than thousands of sabre-toothed tigers on the loose around Rottingdean.

"I can only draw stick men," mumbled

Hardeep, and we all agreed that would have been a bit rubbish.

"I'd have drawn a huge slab of white chocolate," Ben Tucker said, and we all agreed that would be cool, but really, who draws huge slabs of white chocolate?

"I'd have drawn *this*," piped up Daisy Horwitz.

We all turned and stared. Daisy had the clicker pen and had scribbled something on her palm. It wasn't a monster or anything like that. It was just three lines – one on top of the other – sticking out of a little cloud shape. It looked like a gust of wind on a weather map.

"Um, Daisy?" I asked. "What is that?"

Her grin spread ever wider, and she held her palm closer for us to see. "It's a massive fart," she said. "I draw them all the time. I'm sort of obsessed. Great big massive farts. Sometimes I even draw little people getting blown away. Just like this…"

"DAISY!" I yelled.

I snatched the pen from her hand. "That's the magic pen! It brings things to life!"

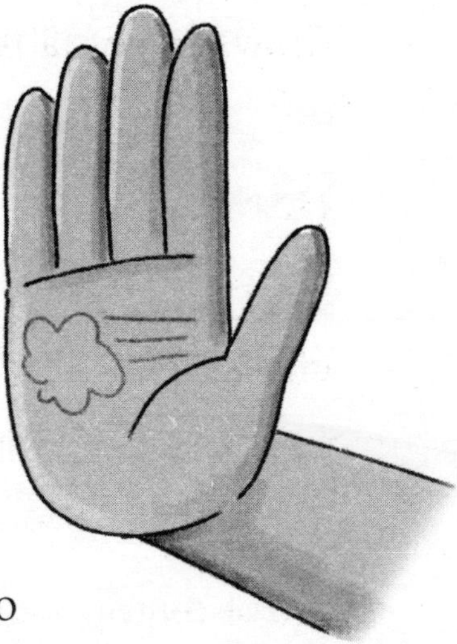

Her eyes went all wide and she snapped her hand shut, trying to hide the thing we'd all just seen.

"It's … it's just a fart," she muttered. "How bad can that be?"

And then it happened.

If I'd had any doubts that the clicker

pen was magical, they were blown away by the biggest and loudest fart in history. It was like thunder and a tornado and a thousand stink bombs all at once, only way louder and way stronger and way stinkier.

The force of it sent us staggering along the street, tumbling into one another. House windows rattled. Tiles slid from roofs and shattered on the pavement. A flock of seagulls that had been flying over us suddenly dropped to the ground – they'd passed out from the stink. It was like a massive giant who'd eaten nothing but cabbage for weeks had dropped his trousers at the end of the street and let rip.

An old man leaned out of his door and screamed, "TAKE COVER, IT'S A MASSIVE FART!", which was pretty clever of him because he hadn't seen Daisy's drawing.

He was wrong about one thing – it wasn't just *a* massive fart. Now there came another, and then another – each louder and grosser and more powerful than the last. Rubbish bins clattered along the street, and a tabby cat, which had picked a bad moment to come out of its cat flap, vomited on its paws.

We scrambled behind a wall and held our noses, as blast after terrible blast swept down the street. Some Army soldiers arrived wearing gas masks, but I guess they had no training in fighting massive farts because in the end they just ran off.

"The care home is only a few streets away," I yelled. "If we link arms, we can fight through the farts to get there. But stay together. We can't leave anyone behind."

"Why not?" Ben Tucker asked.

"Well, it's just not nice, is it?"

Everyone nodded, agreeing that it wasn't nice at all. Then we set off, hand in hand, spreading our human chain across the street. Heads down and breaths held, we fought against the massive farts as

they tried to blast us back. Step by step, we carried on, stopping only to cry things like, "IT'S SO GROSS!" or "IT SMELLS LIKE ONE OF MY DAD'S!" or "I JUST SWALLOWED SOME!" or "YOU CAN'T SWALLOW A FART!" or "DON'T TELL ME I CAN'T BECAUSE I JUST DID!"

I spotted an adult staring at us from a window. His mouth hung open in astonishment and I thought I saw respect –

even admiration – in his eyes. But then he opened the window and yelled, "Why are you kids walking into a massive fart?"

There was no time to reply – we staggered to the end of the street, through the gushing gusts, and then broke into a run all the way to the care home.

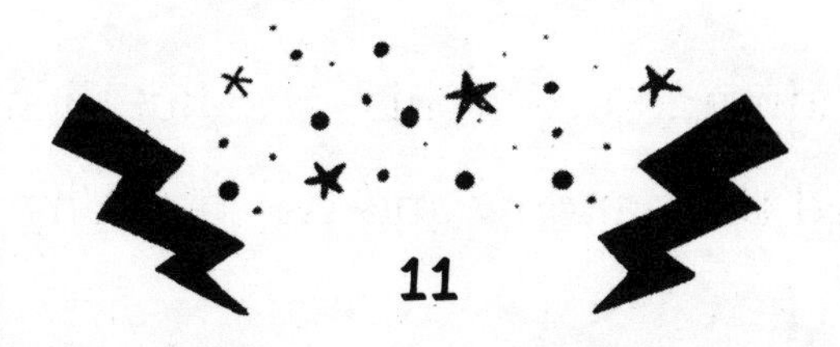

11

THE PEOPLE WHO'VE LIVED FOR QUITE A LONG TIME

The Rottingdean care home used to be called the Rottingdean Old People's Home, but calling people old is rude, so the name got changed to the Rottingdean Home for People Who've Lived for Quite a Long Time. That was a bit of a mouthful, so it was changed again to the Rottingdean Home for Folk of Considerable Age, but no one could spell the word "considerable". They decided "ancient" sounded more respectful, so

they changed it to the Rottingdean Home for Ancient People. Only, that turned out to be the rudest name of them all, but they'd run out of space on the sign, so now no one has a clue what it's called. Dad says the residents probably can't read the sign anyway, because of their bad eyesight. Mum said that was mean and we should just call it a care home because that sounds nice.

The care home has the best spot in town – halfway up the Downs, overlooking the sea in one direction and hills in the other. But it's a pretty ugly building. It looks like a giant brick shoe box, except it's full of old people rather than shoes.

As we approached, an Army plane blasted over us and we covered our ears against the noise. When we uncovered them, we heard something else…

Chanting?

It sounded like some sort of ceremony was happening inside. Firelight flickered off the windows, so bright it dazzled our eyes.

"What's going on in there?" Suzie muttered.

We found out as soon as we stepped inside.

The six of us stood in the reception area, staring in astonishment. The People Who'd Lived for Quite a Long Time were doing some sort of ritual. They wore long red robes with hoods up, and stood in a circle around a fire, chanting in some ancient language.

It was weird because:

- They were holding a secret ritual, which is quite weird no matter what.
- They had lit a bonfire in the middle of the residents' lounge, burning a pile of *Radio Times* and *Reader's Digest* magazines, which is definitely against health-and-safety rules.
- They were doing it so *well*.

I know you're not meant to make assumptions about old people, but these old people were *properly* old. Even so, they were chanting really loudly and banging things on the ground, and totally giving it their all. One guy – who must have been at least a hundred and fifty – waved his Zimmer frame in the air, calling on some ancient god for something or other. Another woman – who was maybe two hundred years old – stood on the reception desk with her arms spread wide, yelling something in what seemed like a long-lost language but, as we edged further inside, we realized was just a load of random words strung together.

"OH GREAT SAUCER BOTTLE SPARROW SHY! WE PRAY NAPKIN NEWSREADER OATS..."

Honestly, it was total gibberish – but it was still awesome. All of the adults in Rottingdean were losing the plot, but these guys were really doing it in style.

"Daisy, which one is your gran?" I asked, shouting above the chanting.

"Over there," Daisy yelled back. "I think she's about to sacrifice herself."

Daisy's gran lay on a table at the front of the lounge. In her wrinkled hands, she was grasping what looked like a toy dagger, which was poised directly over her heart. She spotted us as we approached, and sat up and grinned.

"Hi, Gran!" Daisy shouted. "What's up?"

Daisy's gran smiled sweetly, the toy dagger still hovering by her chest. "Hello, sweetie," she replied. "We're welcoming our new masters. Don't you know we're about to be enslaved by monsters from another dimension?"

"Actually, we're on a quest to stop all that," Suzie replied.

"That sounds dangerous," Daisy's gran said. "How can I help?"

I took the magical clicker pen from my pocket. "Do you recognize this?" I asked.

She swung her legs over the edge of the table and put on a pair of thick-lensed glasses that made her eyes look all huge like a lizard's. They grew even huger as she stared at the pen.

Finally, she sighed and raised a hand.

The chanting stopped, and everyone in the lounge turned to watch us.

"I've been waiting for this day," Daisy's gran said. "Although I never expected it would be my own grandchild who would come for me after all these years."

Her grip tightened on the toy dagger and she thrust it towards us. We all jumped back saying, "WHOA!" and stuff like that.

The weapon trembled in her hand. "Now I am torn between family and my duty to the ancient gods of—"

She stopped talking and leaned closer, squinting again at the pen in my hand. "Oh," she said. "Oh no, sorry. I thought that was something else."

She quickly tucked the dagger away under her gown.

"So you *don't* recognize it?" I asked.

She shrugged. "Looks like a pen."

"This pen could be the key to saving the world," Suzie explained. "It came from this place. You won it in the raffle here, then gave it to Daisy for her birthday, remember?"

Daisy's gran nodded, as if that sounded about right. She called to the other residents, who were all staring at us.

"Does anybody recognize this kid's pen?"

Most of the residents shuffled forward, putting on their own glasses. They stared at the pen I was holding up. Finally, a hunched old man at the side of the room raised a shaky hand.

"I have been waiting for this day..." he croaked.

"Have you really, though?" I asked.

"No," he mumbled, lowering his hand. "I don't even know what day it is."

"Has anyone *actually* been waiting for this day?" I asked.

Huge round eyes stared back at me blankly from behind thick lenses.

"Is anyone here a wizard?" I asked.

Everyone's hand went up.

"Is anyone here *really* a wizard?" I asked.

Everyone's hand went down.

"Is anyone a fairy? Or a genie?" Ben Tucker called.

"I think I might be a genie," one of the residents rasped.

"Have you ever lived in a bottle?" Suzie asked.

"I can't remember."

"I think she would remember living in a bottle," Suzie whispered to me.

I groaned. This wasn't going well. "Is anyone a magical unicorn?" I continued. "A gnome? A warlock? A witch?"

"Wait! Wait! Yes!"

Another hand shot up. This time it was Daisy's gran, who grinned so wide that her false teeth dropped out. She popped them back in.

"You're a witch, Gran?" Daisy asked.

"Oh no, sweetie, I *was* a witch."

"When?"

"A few weeks ago."

"You were a witch until a few weeks ago?" Jago asked.

"No, I *was* a witch a few weeks ago. For about twenty minutes."

"Can you be a witch for just twenty minutes?" I asked.

Daisy's gran shrugged. "I was just practising from a book. It seemed like a nice hobby, but there was a lot to read and my eyesight isn't so good. I cast a few spells before I got tired and gave up. I took up fencing instead."

I looked at Jago and the others, and we all smiled. This could be what we were looking for.

"One of those spells must have worked," Suzie suggested.

"Do you remember casting a spell to bring drawings to life?" I asked Daisy's gran.

"My dear, I barely remember what I had for breakfast," she replied. "I didn't think there could be any harm in it. The book said that the spells were reversible. You just have to read them backwards."

This was brilliant news!

"So we just have to get hold of the book and read the spell backwards?" I asked. "That will reverse the magic and all the monsters will vanish?"

"If you say so, my dear," she mumbled.

"Great! So where's the book?"

Daisy's gran's grin changed to a grimace. "Ah, that is the challenge. The spell book lies far away in a distant land. High up on a mountain there is a cave known as the Lair of the Deathwalkers. If you can defeat the Deathwalkers, you then must scale the Wall of Unutterable Doom. The spell book sits at the top, guarded by an invisible dragon that you must defeat in a board game of its choice. Only then will it grant you access to the Realm of the Written

Word, where you will find the tome that you seek."

My heart sank. A few of our gang groaned.

"That seems unnecessarily complicated," I muttered.

Daisy's gran shrugged. "These things often are."

"It's just that we don't have much time. Is there another way we can find this Realm of the Written Word place?"

She popped a mint humbug in her mouth. "Oh, yes," she said. "It's the local library."

"You mean Rottingdean Library?" I asked.

"Yep."

This was amazing news! We thanked Daisy's gran and rushed from the room. Just before we left, she called out again.

"Wait!"

We turned. She had pulled up her hood and was glaring at us from its shadow. Her voice had gone all croaky and mysterious, too. "If you seek the Realm of the Written Word, there is one more thing you must know..."

This didn't sound good...

"It closes at three p.m. on Wednesdays," she said.

"Thanks, Gran!" Daisy called, and we all bundled out of the door.

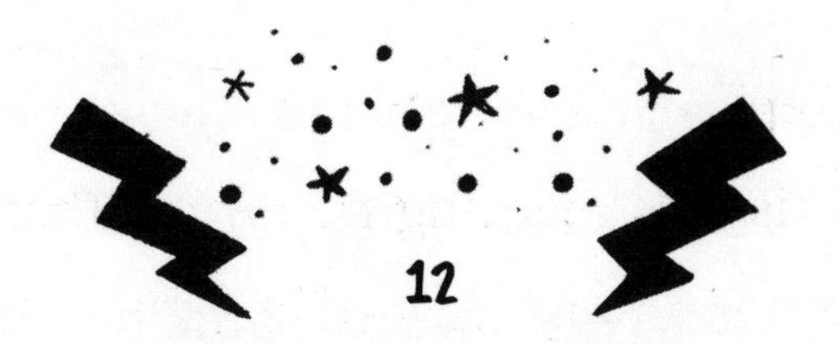

12

WE DON'T HAVE MUCH TIME

We didn't have much time. Not only were thousands of flying great white sharks about to destroy our town, but also the library was closing in half an hour. We knew we didn't have much time. *Obviously* we didn't have much time. But everyone still kept telling us we didn't have much time.

An Army jeep sped past headed for the coast. One of the soldiers yelled at us as it went by, "Get inside! You don't have much time!"

A fire engine went screaming by, and a firefighter shouted, "Hey, kids, what's the time?" Then, when we told him, he yelled, "You don't have much time!"

Some random guy even stuck his head out of his window as we ran by, and shouted, "Hey slow down! You have loads of time. No, wait, my watch is broken. You hardly have any!"

"We know!" I yelled.

We were running as fast as we could, down the hill towards the local library. Alarms wailed, sirens, um, also wailed and car horns honked as people sat in traffic jams, trying to flee the town. We could see the sharks now, flying over Rottingdean beach propelled by wide sweeps of their tails. They were MASSIVE and they were all grinning, showing off weird green lips and rows of razor-sharp teeth. As we watched, neon-pink laser beams blasted from their eyes. All around Rottingdean, things began to melt – traffic signs, the slide in the fun park, the plastic fisherman outside Frying Nemo…

"Seriously, Jago," Suzie yelled, "why'd it have to be great white sharks?"

"Easy to draw," Jago replied, and we all agreed it was a reasonable answer.

Only, it wasn't *just* great white sharks. Further along the coast, a towering figure waded through the waves breaking on the beach. The monster looked a bit like a human, except that it was taller than a really tall house and covered in green moss.

"What is *that*?" Hardeep cried.

"That's a giant troll with infinite eyes," Jago replied. "It throws its eyeballs at people and they explode."

As we watched, the troll pulled out one of its eyeballs and hurled it at a hut on the beach. There was a small explosion, and the hut collapsed in a pile of smoking woodwork. Now something else moved through the smoke, marching across the shore. It was half the size of the troll, but twice as fast – a blur of movement and metal.

"Now what's *that*?" shrieked Ben Tucker.

"A giant ninja robot," Jago replied. "Really dangerous."

The soldiers on the beach began firing their big cannon things at the monsters and black smoke swirled around the coast. The police were down there, too, but weren't being much help – they just waved truncheons at the sharks and the ninja robot and the giant troll with infinite exploding eyes, as if to give them all a good telling-off. That didn't last long, because they were all sent tumbling by another of Daisy's mega farts that blasted across the beach, stinking them all out.

It was absolute chaos – but, well, pretty cool to see. Hopefully, though, it would be over soon; we'd reached the library, and – fingers crossed – were about to find a way to end the end of the world.

"Hey, you kids!" a police officer hollered as we threw open the library door. "You don't have much time!"

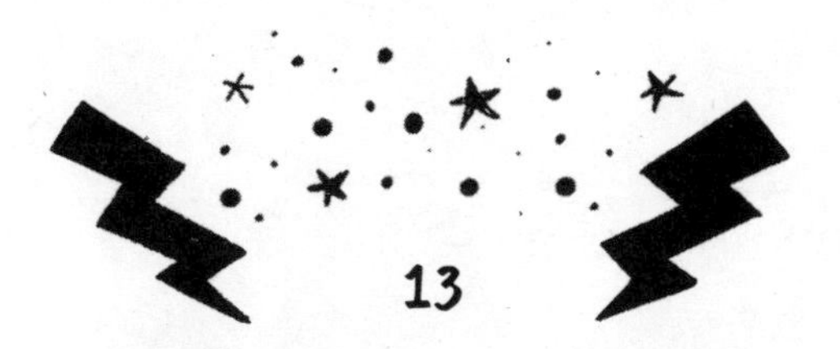

13

THE REALM OF THE WRITTEN WORD (AKA THE LOCAL LIBRARY)

"How can I help?"

The librarian smiled at us and closed her laptop as, outside the building, the world began to end. Explosions along the shore shook the library walls, causing books to tumble from their shelves. The windows rattled, and the librarian's desk jolted. But she just smiled sweetly.

"Are you looking for a good story, or perhaps something to help with your homework?" she asked.

"Have you not noticed? There's a Monster Apocalypse going on outside!"

"Libraries have been threatened by worse things," she replied.

"Really? What like?" Daisy asked.

"The government. They're shutting down all the libraries."

"Wow," Suzie said. "You mean the

government are closing libraries down rather than improving them to make them even more useful to the millions of people across the country who rely on them? I'm sorry, that sucks."

We all agreed, that really did suck. But, for now, we had to focus on the monster-sized problem outside. Or, rather, the tens of thousands of monster-sized problems with laser-beam eyes…

"We're trying to stop the end of the world," Suzie said.

"That sounds dangerous," the librarian replied. "How can I help?"

"We need to find a book of spells," I explained. "Daisy's gran got it here."

"Enchantments?" the librarian asked. "Incantations? Earth spells?"

“Spells that make drawings come to life.”

“Ah. You’ll find that in aisle six, under ‘Spells that make drawings come to life’.”

We thanked her and had begun to run towards aisle six when another explosion caused more books to slide from the shelves. The doors burst open and a dozen soldiers charged in. Some of them hid under tables. Others pretended to *be* tables, so no one would notice them hiding. One wild-eyed soldier grabbed Ben Tucker and screamed **“GET OUT THERE AND FIGHT!”** before scuttling behind a plant pot.

I yanked Ben away and we bumped into the **BIGBUM** scientist, who was waving her **Strange Scientific Device** around, shrieking, "They're everywhere! They're all around us!"

Next, Suzie's mum stumbled in. She was sobbing and laughing at the same time so her face was all twisted up and streaked with tears. She was grabbing soldiers and pulling at their noses to see if they were wearing masks.

"Are you Ant?" she cried. "Are you Dec? Where are the cameras? Please, tell me where the cameras are!"

My own parents came rushing into the library next. I thought they were searching for us, but it turned out Mum was just looking for a Wi-Fi signal for her Zoom meeting. Dad was still in a total panic, charging around, bouncing off the shelves like the ball in a pinball machine.

PASSWORD

He ran past a TV that was broadcasting live from the prime minister's bunker. On the screen was an empty seat. The prime minister had fled his own survival bunker.

For a moment, all of us kids just stood watching the chaos. Then we all said exactly the same thing at exactly the same time:

"All the adults are freaking out."

It was up to us now.

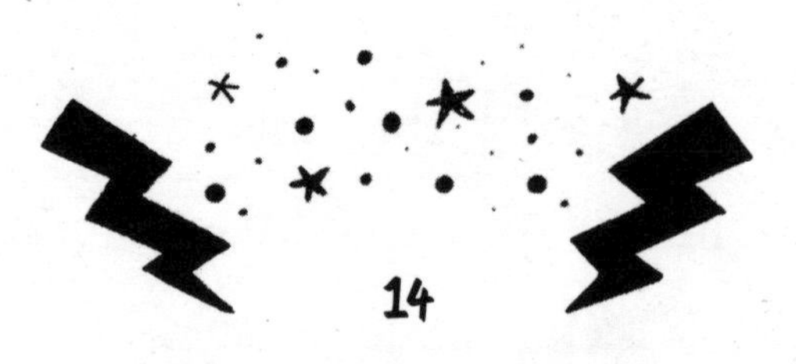

14
THE SPELL BOOK

"Over here!" Suzie called.

She waved to us from one of the library aisles and we rushed over, weaving between panicking adults. She'd found the books about spells. Only, there were dozens of them crammed into the shelf. We moved along, reading the titles on the spines:

SPELLS TO MAKE WASPS GO AWAY

INCANTATIONS TO GET RID OF ANNOYING STONES IN YOUR SHOES

CHARMS TO MAKE IT LOOK LIKE YOU'VE EATEN ALL YOUR DINNER WHEN YOU DON'T LIKE THE THING YOU'VE BEEN COOKED

SPELLS TO MAKE SPELLS WORK BETTER

"These are surprisingly specific," Hardeep muttered.

"So which one did my gran read?" Daisy asked.

Another blast caused the shelves to shake and more books to spill onto the floor. One of them landed by my feet.

I stared at the title on the front. "Guys ... I think I've found it."

I picked up the book and showed the gang. The title, which was very long, had been crammed onto the cover in super-tiny letters:

SPELLS FOR
PEOPLE WHO
HAVE LIVED FOR
QUITE A LONG
TIME AND FANCY
A NEW HOBBY BUT
DON'T WANT TO
PUT TOO MUCH
EFFORT INTO
ANYTHING MUCH

I laid the book on a table and we gathered around it, turning the pages to search for a spell Daisy's gran might have used to make Jago's clicker pen magical. But now the library darkened, as something blocked the sunlight streaming in through the windows.

"It's right above us!" one of the soldiers yelled, looking out of a window. "A giant robot that seems to be an expert in kung fu!"

"It's ninjutsu!" Jago yelled. "And it's about to kick the roof off!"

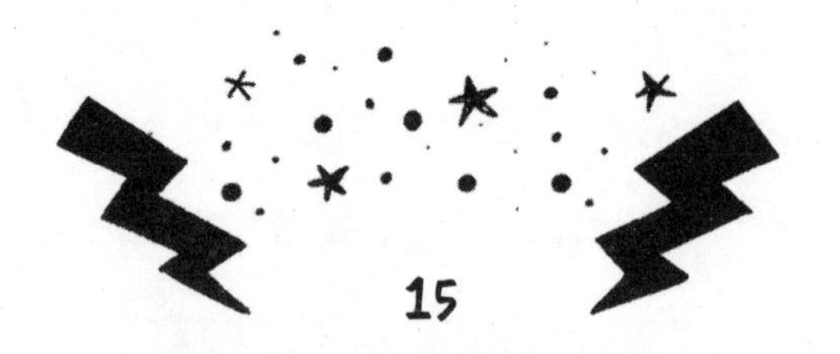

15

THE LIBRARIAN VS THE MONSTERS

Can you imagine a giant ninja robot trying to kick a library roof off?

We all dropped to the ground shouting things like, "YAAAA!" and "WAAAAA!" and "ACTUALLY, THAT LOOKED MORE LIKE A KUNG FU KICK THAN A NINJA KICK, BUT WHATEVER!" as books and shelves crashed down around us. At the same time, a blast of the mega fart rushed through the building, sweeping up books and carrying them off like leaves in a really stinky tornado.

Above the library, dozens of great white sharks flew across the sky. And then something else appeared. Something five times the size of the giant ninja robot. Something covered in tangled hair and grubby green moss. Something that basically looked like a massive angry bush.

"It's the troll with infinite eyes!" one of the soldiers shrieked.

"Seriously, how could you know it's called that?" Jago cried.

"Just looks like one," the soldier yelled back.

I yanked my brother with me under a table, as the troll reached a scraggly hand and plucked out one of its eyeballs. Another eye immediately appeared in the empty socket, and the troll grinned, showing off teeth that looked like wonky gravestones. It was just about to hurl the exploding eyeball into the library when a voice called out from close by.

"Excuse me!"

The troll grunted.

"I said, *excuse me*."

It was the librarian. She stood among the ruins, glaring up at the mean old troll.

"It is five past three," she said. "The library is now closed."

The troll's hairy face screwed up tight. I thought it was about to throw the eyeball at her, but instead it turned its wrist and lifted some hair to check its watch.

"Oh," it said. "Sorry. I'll come back tomorrow."

Then it stomped off!

The giant robot seemed to have ninja-d off, and the sharks had flown past, too. But suddenly, none of that mattered. I scrambled from our hiding place, staring around the chaos. Something else had disappeared, too.

"The spell book!" I gasped.

It was gone!

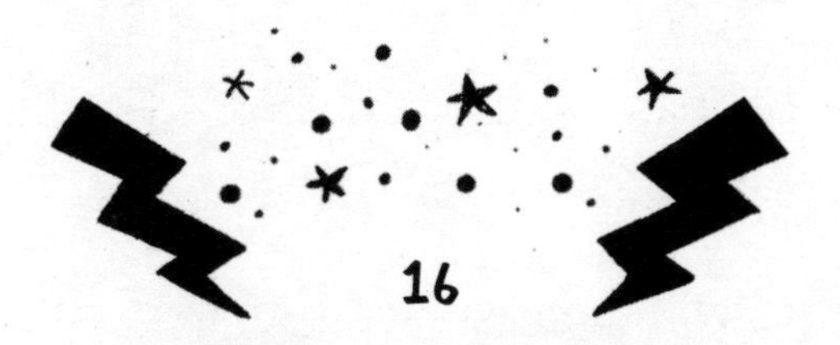

16

WHAT CHAOS REALLY MEANS

I just looked back through this story, and I've used the word "chaos" quite a lot. The thing is, each time I really meant it. But "chaos" is a tricky word, because adults freaking out really *does* look like chaos – until you've seen your town being pulverized by thousands of monsters drawn by your little brother. Then you know what chaos *really* means.

We stood outside the library, staring at the, um, chaos.

"It's chaos," Suzie said.

"It actually *is* this time," Daisy agreed.

The sharks and the troll and the ninja robot and the mega fart were destroying stuff everywhere we looked. The Home for

the People Who've Lived for Quite a Long Time was in ruins, but the residents were continuing their ritual outside, holding up signs saying, WE WELCOME OUR NEW MASTERS and WILL WE STILL

GET FREE BUS PASSES?

"Can anyone see the book?" I called.

"Which book?" Jago asked.

I stared at him. "Seriously?"

"Oh, the *spell* book," he muttered.

"Over there!" Suzie yelled.

There it was, beyond several piles of rubble, perched on a swing in what was left of the fun park.

"There's no way we can reach it," Hardeep said. "We'll be ninja-kicked by the giant robot."

"Or blown up by a troll's eyeball," Daisy suggested.

"Or melted by a flying shark," Ben added.

Or suffocated to death by a massive fart, I thought, but I didn't want to add to the list.

They were right, we'd never get to the book without help. But the Army and the police had fled. We could see their jeeps and vans in a jam on the road out of the town. The helicopters and fighter planes had flown off, too. In fact, the only person defending Rottingdean was old Mrs Liphook, who stood on top of Frying Nemo waving her fly swatter at the sharks in the sky.

"Maybe we don't need the adults," I said. "I mean, they haven't been much help until now. We got this far together, us kids. And kids have one thing that adults don't..."

"We eat our own snot?" Hardeep suggested.

"We burst into tears when someone else gets a present?" Daisy said.

"We walk in on other people in the loo?" Suzie guessed.

"Those are really specific answers," I replied. "What I meant was that we have big imaginations."

"You mean … we'll *pretend* to reach it?" Jago asked.

"No, we'll use our imaginations to *actually* reach it. That's what caused all this in the first place, isn't it – Jago's drawings? So let's do *more* drawings with the magic pen. Only, this time we'll create things to *stop* the monsters so I can reach the spell book."

A tingle ran through my body that had nothing to do with me needing a wee. This was our moment. We didn't *need* adults! We were kids – we could do anything!

I thrust an arm triumphantly in the air.

"Who's with me?" I called.

They all stared at me.

"Why didn't we just do that ages ago?" Suzie asked.

"Eh?"

"Why didn't we draw things to stop the monsters ages ago?" Ben Tucker said. "It seems like an obvious plan."

"I dunno," I muttered. "I only just had the idea..."

We rushed around and grabbed whatever we could find to draw on – scraps of paper, sweet wrappers and boxes blown about by the mega fart. I took the magic pen from my pocket and handed it to my brother.

"So what should we draw?" he asked.

"Whatever you can think of to stop the monsters."

"What if we can't think of anything?" Hardeep said.

"Course you can," I replied. "We're kids, right? This is what we do best. Let's go!"

I set off over the rubble from the buildings, scrambling towards the book. My heart was pounding like mad, but I knew my friends had my back. We'd come this far together. They wouldn't let me down now. Not when we could finally defeat these—

I stopped and looked back.

None of them were drawing anything.

"Guys?" I yelled. "Like, NOW?"

"Oh!" Suzie called. "We weren't quite sure when to start. So, like, now?"

"Yes!"

But it was already too late. A huge shadow loomed over me – a shark-shaped shadow. (It was a flying shark, just in case the shape of the shadow didn't make that clear.) The monster's eyes glowed dazzling red…

I was about to be melted!

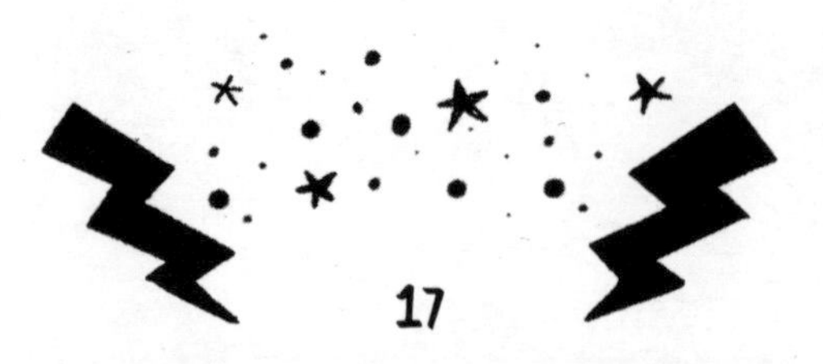

17

WHAT CHAOS ACTUALLY REALLY MEANS

A fizzing laser beam shot from the eyes of the great white shark, aimed straight at me. I covered my head with my arms and screamed, certain I was about to be melted. My scream turned into a … well, a louder scream, as I felt the laser hit my arms. It was searing hot and… liquid … and *milky and sweet…*

I unpeeled my arms

from my head as more creamy-white gloop slid down my face and over my lips. It was weirdly tasty.

"White chocolate..." I mumbled.

I looked up and cried out in joy. Hovering above me, blocking the shark's laser beam, was a huge slab of white chocolate. It was wider than a mattress and thicker than a, um, mattress, and it was melting slowly as it shielded me from the laser, like a deliciously sticky umbrella.

I turned to see my friends, who were all grinning at me with delight. Ben Tucker had the magic pen. He'd drawn exactly what he said he would – his favourite chocolate snack. In fact, he'd drawn dozens of bars. They floated below the sharks, shielding Rottingdean from the flying monsters.

Close by, people were emerging from their hiding places, excited by the falling streams of hot chocolate where the giant white slabs were being hit by laser beams. The adults grinned and laughed, as if a nice bit of chocolate was all they'd needed to solve the problem of the end of the world.

One of the giant chocolate bars shot out to sea, as the troll swatted it away with a hairy fist. The monster spotted me and grinned, and then began to stomp closer. It reached to pull out one of its exploding eyeballs... And then stopped and grunted.

Something had stuck into its hand. It looked like a twig.

Now another twig shot up and dug into the troll's lip. The monster's grunt turned into a groan and then a furious roar, as more and more twig-like things fired from below and stuck into its body. And then something *really weird* happened.

A stick man appeared.

A proper actual stick man, like you'd draw in a doodle. The height of a normal adult, it carried a stick bow and stick arrows. It fired another at the troll, as hundreds more stick men scurried over

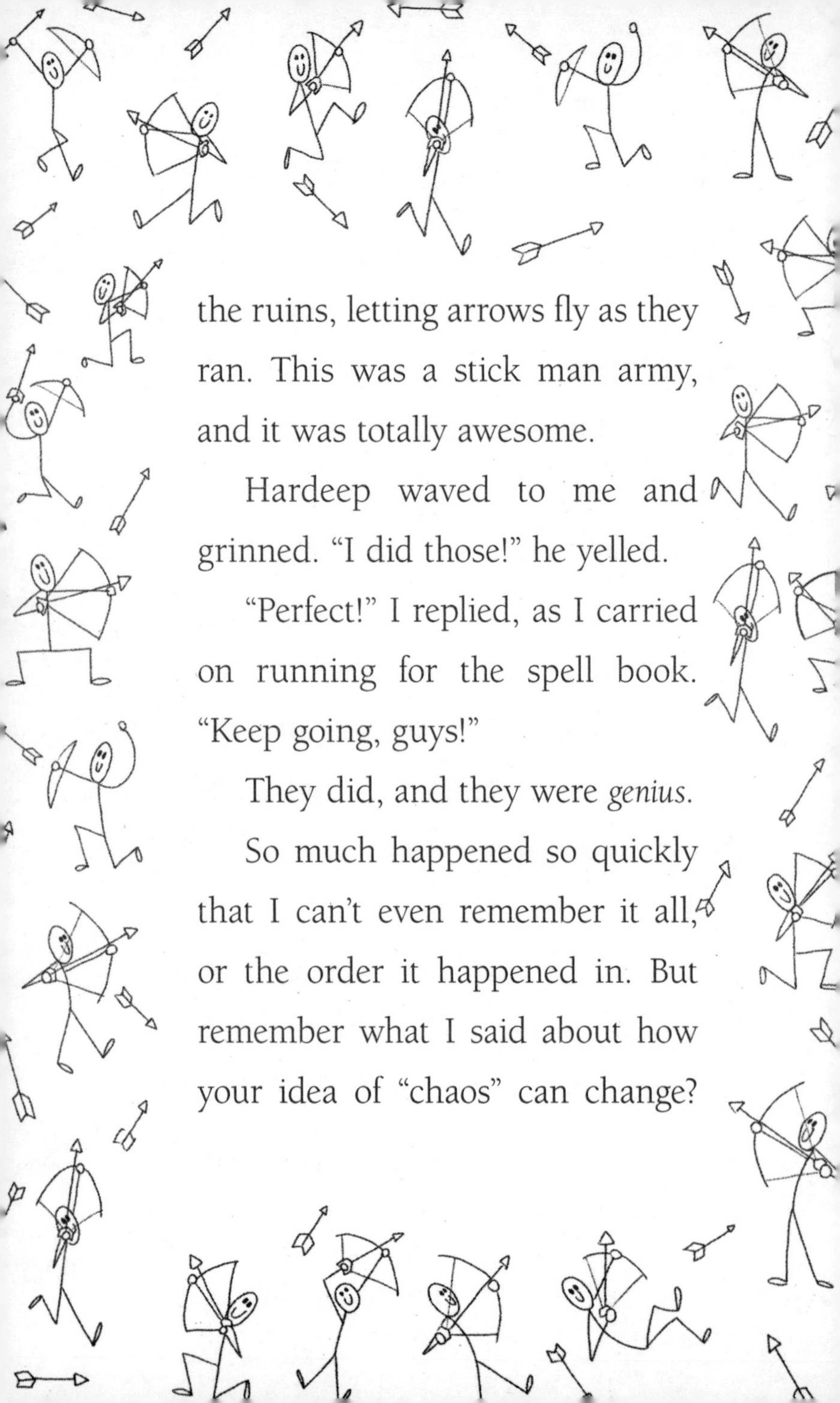

the ruins, letting arrows fly as they ran. This was a stick man army, and it was totally awesome.

Hardeep waved to me and grinned. "I did those!" he yelled.

"Perfect!" I replied, as I carried on running for the spell book. "Keep going, guys!"

They did, and they were *genius*.

So much happened so quickly that I can't even remember it all, or the order it happened in. But remember what I said about how your idea of "chaos" can change?

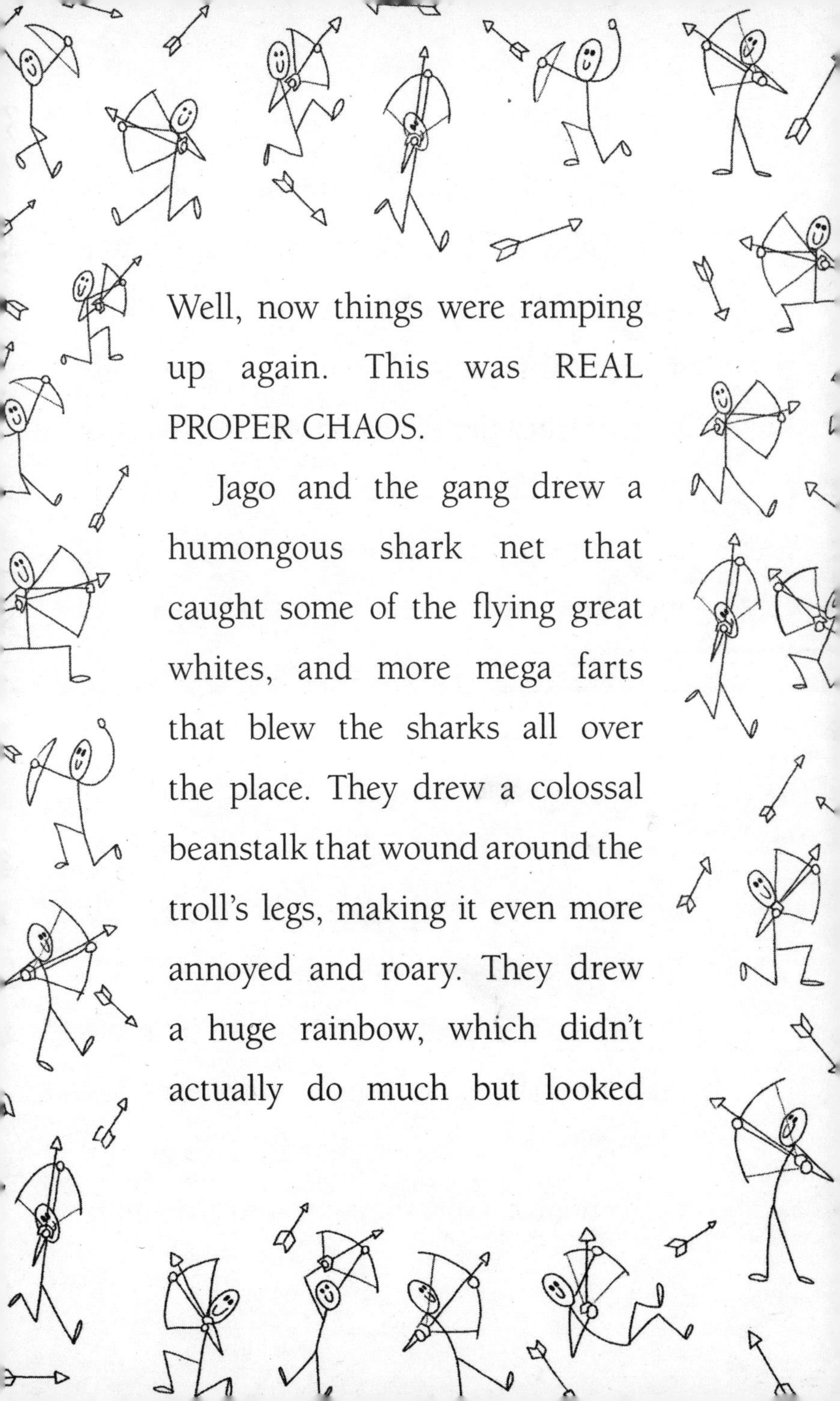

Well, now things were ramping up again. This was REAL PROPER CHAOS.

Jago and the gang drew a humongous shark net that caught some of the flying great whites, and more mega farts that blew the sharks all over the place. They drew a colossal beanstalk that wound around the troll's legs, making it even more annoyed and roary. They drew a huge rainbow, which didn't actually do much but looked pretty. They drew a massive birthday cake, almost the size of the whole town, which fell on top of us in one huge SPLAT and put out most of the fires. Then there was another SPLAT as an equally massive pink jelly landed on everyone. That didn't stop the monsters, but some of the adults had shouted for jelly with their cake, so my friends let them have some.

And then came the best drawing of them all – another giant robot. That may sound crazy when one was bad enough, but my gang had had a brilliant idea. This new robot was a giant KUNG FU robot, and everybody knows that ninjas and kung fu experts are sworn enemies. So the kung fu robot charged straight for the ninja one and they got into this giant robot martial arts battle. They punched and kicked and... Well, they just punched and kicked, really, but in loads of amazing ways. The ninja robot totally forgot about us, and the two robots staggered out to sea, fighting the whole way.

Honestly, it was absolutely awesome.

While the monsters were distracted, I clambered over the ruins and finally reached the spell book. I held it up so my friends could see, but they were all busy drawing new things to fight the monsters. I know we were in a mad rush, but for a moment I just watched them, and it felt pretty cool. All the adults were freaking out; but us kids had got it done.

I opened the spell book and flicked through the pages to a chapter that was helpfully titled "The Chapter You've Been Looking For". I was expecting a long, complicated spell full of long complicated words in ancient languages. But all it said was this:

"HOCUS POCUS"

"Seriously?" I muttered. "That's it?"

My surprise gave way to delight – at last, some luck! All I had to do was read those two simple words backwards – SUCOP SUCOH? – and … and…

Far out at sea, something new had appeared. Something new and huge … and headed this way.

"Um, guys?" I called. "What *is* that?"

"Jago drew it," Hardeep hollered. "We couldn't stop him."

"Jago!" I cried. "What did you draw?"

It was a bit confusing at first. I had to tilt my head and squint and guess at some bits, but after a few seconds, I was able to work it out.

It wasn't good – it was the biggest monster so far.

"Jago!" I shouted. "Is that a mega-sized T-Rex with fighter-plane wings, giant gorilla arms, massive snakes sprouting from its shoulders with cannons on their heads, and poisonous spikes all over its body that it can fire at people with uncannily accurate aim?"

"It's also got a cat's butt," Jago replied, proudly.

"Of course it has," I sighed.

The rest of our gang saw it, too, and, screamed at me to read the spell.

Anyway, you don't really need to know what happened next. In short, I read the spell backwards and there was all this crazy lightning and thunder and the sky glowed red. Then this inter-dimensional black hole appeared over Rottingdean and all the monsters got sucked up through it. Only, the new one – the T-Rex with all the stuff on it – was so huge that the black hole struggled to suck it up, and the monster got so close to me that I saw my face reflected in its shiny teeth, until just at the final second the inter-dimensional black hole won! The last thing we all saw of it, as it got sucked up with an epic roar, was that it really *did* have a cat's butt.

And that was about it, really.

Oh, there was one other thing…

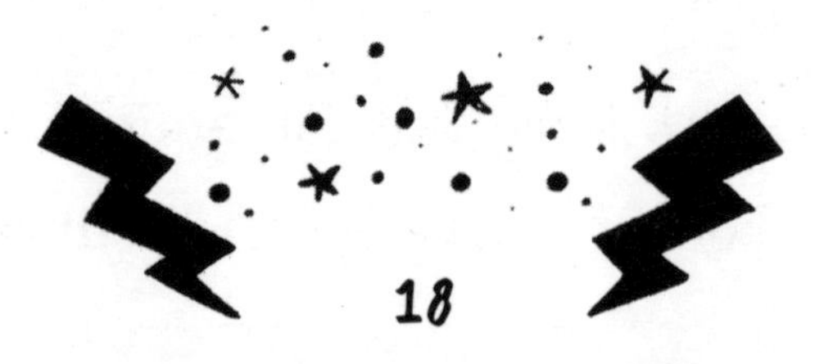

18

THE ONE OTHER THING

By the time the Monster Apocalypse was over and everyone was safe, some of the news helicopters had flown back, and the Army and police had begun to return as well. All the adults came out of hiding, hugging and slapping each other on the back and saying things like, "WE DID IT!" and "THREE CHEERS FOR ALL THE ADULTS!" and "WE KEPT OUR COOL AND DIDN'T FREAK OUT AT ALL."

Me and my brother and Suzie and the rest of our gang sat outside Frying

Nemo, drinking handfuls of melted white chocolate that we'd scooped off the ground.

But, as we watched, the adults did that thing that adults like to do – they looked around for someone to blame. It all happened really fast. Some of the parents complained to Sergeant Snelling, who called over the soldiers, who remembered seeing us kids with the pen and the spell book… And just like that, we were guilty, apparently.

Incredible. Not a single adult had believed us when we were trying to warn them. But now that they needed someone to blame, they had it totally sussed out.

Sergeant Snelling marched over to us, with a crowd of adults following.

"We have reason to believe that all of this was caused by you children," he snapped.

One of the soldiers butted in. His face was as red as a really red, red balloon, and spit sprayed from his mouth as he yelled, "YOU WILL ALL BE TAKEN TO A HIGH-SECURITY MILITARY PRISON ON A REMOTE ROCKY ISLAND, WHERE YOU WILL REMAIN IN SOLITARY CONFINEMENT FOR THE REST OF YOUR LIVES IN CELLS CARVED INTO UNDERGROUND CAVES."

"That seems unnecessarily complicated," Ben Tucker said.

"THESE THINGS OFTEN ARE."

The soldier turned and smiled sweetly at our parents, who had gathered behind him. "Of course I'll need your permission to imprison your children in such a dangerous place for the rest of their lives."

They all shrugged.

"Fine by us," one of them said.

"Seems fair enough," another agreed. "And totally legal."

"Did you say 'a remote rocky island'?" my mum asked.

I sat up, pleased that she, at least, was challenging this gross injustice. But then my heart sank.

"If I visit, will there be Wi-Fi?" she asked.

This really wasn't good. As the parents began to finalize the details for our imprisonments, I stared at the spell book in my hands. I was about to open it and shout a spell at random, hoping it might do something weird to make the adults panic again. But there was no need, because Suzie Grotwood had a plan, too, and it was totally, utterly genius.

She stood up and burped the whole alphabet!

It was AMAZING! For the first time ever, she did it all in one whole burp, and all the adults went completely nuts. In an instant, everyone forgot all about how we'd almost caused the end of the world and went mad for Suzie's achievement. Some people cheered. Others clapped and shouted hip-hip-hoorays. One of the news helicopters captured it live, so everyone all over the country saw it, too. Then the news spread all over the world, and suddenly Suzie was one of the biggest stars on the planet. She made a FORTUNE appearing on TV shows doing her alphabet burp. They even made a blockbuster movie about how it happened, which became the biggest box office hit of all time and won every single award, including some that weren't even for movies.

Anyway, Suzie used some of her fortune to rebuild Rottingdean exactly how it was. Some of the locals said that she might have rebuilt it a little *better* than it was, and I get their point, but at least everything is back to normal now.

As for me and Jago – well, we wrote this story! Actually, our dad helped, too, but his parts were rubbish so we took most of them out. All of it is true, apart from the stuff we made up. Oh, and we left out the bit when the monsters came back, only much bigger, and turned half of all humans into slaves in another dimension, until humanity fought back and regained its freedom in an epic war. It kinda felt repetitive, and didn't involve me and my brother, anyway – because we managed to sleep through the whole thing.

AUTHOR'S NOTE

Remember when we were all stuck at home and parents had to do homeschooling? I freaked out, convinced my sons Otis and Jago would discover how terrible I am at most subjects. To hide my failings, I asked them to make up a story, which I'd help them write. At that time Jago was drawing weird monsters all over the place. Otis had the idea of linking them into a story – this story. Most of the ideas here are theirs, and they're WAY better than any I could have had. Really, this book is a celebration of their imaginations, and of your imagination. Next time you're wondering what to do, look around you, see what you see, and turn it into the silliest story you possibly can.

Oh, and can you not tell Otis and Jago that authors get paid for writing books?

ROB LLOYD JONES is the author of the highly acclaimed middle-grade novels *Wild Boy* and *Wild Boy and the Black Terror*, as well as four titles in the Jake Atlas adventure series. This is his first story for younger readers, created with his sons, Otis (9) and Jago (5), during homeschooling. Rob lives in East Sussex with his wife, and monster-mad Otis and Jago.

ALEX PATRICK's lifelong love for cartoons, picture books and comics has shaped him into the passionate children's illustrator he is today. Alex loves creating original, humorous characters, and is often found laughing to himself as he draws picture books such as *Glamingo* and *Be Happy*. Alex lives in Kent.

IF YOU LOVED ME, MY BROTHER AND THE MONSTER MELTDOWN, TRY THESE OTHER BONKERS BOOKS!